TRUMAN
CAPOTE

FIRST AND LAST

PENGUIN BOOKS

PENGUIN BOOKS

Published by the Penguin Group. Penguin Books Ltd, 27 Wrights Lane,
London W8 5TZ, England. Penguin Books USA Inc., 375 Hudson Street,
New York, New York 10014, USA. Penguin Books Australia Ltd, Ringwood,
Victoria, Australia. Penguin Books Canada Ltd, 10 Alcorn Avenue, Toronto,
Ontario, Canada M4V 3B2. Penguin Books (NZ) Ltd, 182–190 Wairau Road,
Auckland 10, New Zealand · Penguin Books Ltd, Registered Offices: Har-
mondsworth, Middlesex, England · **'Master Misery'** is taken from *A Tree of
Night and Other Stories* and **'La Côte Basque'** from *Answered Prayers*,
published by Penguin Books in 1967 and 1993 respectively. This edition
published 1995 · Copyright © 1949 by Truman Capote. Copyright © The Estate
of Truman Capote, 1986. All rights reserved · Typeset by Datix International
Limited, Bungay, Suffolk. Printed in England by Clays Ltd, St Ives plc · Except
in the United States of America, this book is sold subject to the condition
that it shall not, by way of trade or otherwise, be lent, re-sold, hired out,
or otherwise circulated without the publisher's prior consent in any form of
binding or cover other than that in which it is published and without a similar
condition including this condition being imposed on the subsequent purchaser ·
10 9 8 7 6 5 4 3 2 1

CONTENTS

Master Misery

Her high heels, clacking across the marble foyer, made her think of ice cubes rattling in a glass, and the flowers, those autumn chrysanthemums in the urn at the entrance, if touched they would shatter, splinter, she was sure, into frozen dust; yet the house was warm, even somewhat overheated, but cold, and Sylvia shivered, but cold, like the snowy swollen wastes of the secretary's face: Miss Mozart, who dressed all in white, as though she were a nurse. Perhaps she really was; that, of course, could be the answer. Mr Revercomb, you are mad, and this is your nurse; she thought about it for a moment: well, no. And now the butler brought her scarf. His beauty touched her: slender, so gentle, a Negro with freckled skin and reddish, unreflecting eyes. As he opened the door, Miss Mozart appeared, her starched uniform rustling drily in the hall. 'We hope you will return,' she said, and handed Sylvia a sealed envelope. 'Mr Revercomb was most particularly pleased.'

Outside, dusk was falling like blue flakes, and

Sylvia walked crosstown along the November streets until she reached the lonely upper reaches of Fifth Avenue. It occurred to her then that she might walk home through the park: an act of defiance almost, for Henry and Estelle, always insistent upon their city wisdom, had said over and again, Sylvia, you have no idea how dangerous it is, walking in the park after dark; look what happened to Myrtle Calisher. This isn't Easton, honey. That was the other thing they said. And said. God, she was sick of it. Still, and aside from a few of the other typists at SnugFare, an underwear company for which she worked, who else in New York did she know? Oh, it would be all right if only she did not have to live with them, if she could afford somewhere a small room of her own; but there in that chintz-cramped apartment she sometimes felt she would choke them both. And why did she come to New York? For whatever reason, and it was indeed becoming vague, a principal cause of leaving Easton had been to rid herself of Henry and Estelle; or rather, their counterparts, though in point of fact Estelle was actually from Easton, a town north of Cincinnati. She and Sylvia had grown up together. The real trouble with Henry and Estelle was that they were so excruciatingly married. Namby-pamby, bootsytotsy, and everything had a name: the telephone was Tinkling Tillie, the sofa, Our Nellie, the bed, Big Bear; yes, and what about those His-Her towels, those He-She pillows? Enough to drive you loony. 'Loony!' she said aloud, the quiet park erasing her voice. It was lovely now, and she was right to have walked here, with wind moving through the leaves, and globe lamps, freshly aglow, kindling the chalk drawings of children, pink birds, blue arrows, green hearts. But suddenly, like a pair of obscene words, there appeared on the path two boys: pimple-faced, grinning, they loomed in the dusk like menacing flames, and Sylvia, passing them, felt a burning all through her, quite as though she'd brushed fire. They turned and followed her past a deserted playground, one of them bump-bumping a stick along an iron fence, the other whistling: these sounds accumulated around her like the gathering roar of an oncoming engine, and when one of the boys, with a laugh, called, 'Hey, whatsa hurry?' her mouth twisted for breath. Don't, she thought, thinking to throw down her purse and run. At that moment, a man walking a dog came up a sidepath, and she followed at his heels to the exit. Wouldn't they feel gratified, Henry and Estelle, wouldn't they

3

we-told-you-so if she were to tell them? And, what is more, Estelle would write it home and the next thing you knew it would be all over Easton that she'd been raped in Central Park. She spent the rest of the way home despising New York: anonymity, its virtuous terror; and the squeaking drainpipe, all-night light, ceaseless footfall, subway corridor, numbered door (3C).

'Shh, honey,' Estelle said, sidling out of the kitchen, 'Bootsy's doing his homework.' Sure enough, Henry, a law student at Columbia, was hunched over his books in the living-room, and Sylvia, at Estelle's request, took off her shoes before tiptoeing through. Once inside her room she threw herself on the bed and put her hands over her eyes. Had today really happened? Miss Mozart and Mr Revercomb, were they really there in the tall house on Seventy-eighth Street?

'So, honey, what happened today?' Estelle had entered without knocking.

Sylvia sat up on her elbow. 'Nothing. Except that I typed ninety-seven letters.'

'About what, honey?' asked Estelle, using Sylvia'a hairbrush.

4   'Oh, hell, what do you suppose? SnugFare, the

shorts that safely support our leaders of Science and Industry.'

'Gee, honey, don't sound so cross. I don't know what's wrong with you sometimes. You sound so cross. Ouch! Why don't you get a new brush? This one's just knotted with hair . . .'

'Mostly yours.'

'What did you say?'

'Skip it.'

'Oh, I thought you said something. Anyway, like I was saying, I wish you didn't have to go to that office and come home every day feeling cross and out of sorts. Personally, and I said this to Bootsy just last night and he agreed with me one hundred per cent, I said, Bootsy, I think Sylvia ought to get married: a girl high-strung like that needs her tensions relaxed. There's no earthly reason why you shouldn't. I mean maybe you're not pretty in the ordinary sense, but you have beautiful eyes, and an intelligent, really sincere look. In fact you're the sort of girl any professional man would be lucky to get. And I should think you would want to . . . Look what a different person I am since I married Henry. Doesn't it make you lonesome seeing how happy we are? I'm here to tell you, honey, that there is nothing like lying in bed at night with a man's arms around you and . . .'

'Estelle! For Christ's sake!' Sylvia sat bolt upright in bed, anger on her cheeks like rouge. But after a moment she bit her lip and lowered her eyelids. 'I'm sorry,' she said, 'I didn't mean to shout. Only I wish you wouldn't talk like that.'

'It's all right,' said Estelle, smiling in a dumb, puzzled way. Then she went over and gave Sylvia a kiss. 'I understand, honey. It's just that you're plain wore out. And I'll bet you haven't had anything to eat either. Come on in the kitchen and I'll scramble you some eggs.'

When Estelle set the eggs before her, Sylvia felt quite ashamed; after all, Estelle was trying to be nice; and so then, as though to make it all up, she said: 'Something did happen today.'

Estelle sat down across from her with a cup of coffee, and Sylvia went on: 'I don't know how to tell about it. It's so odd. But – well, I had lunch at the Automat today, and I had to share the table with these three men. I might as well have been invisible because they talked about the most personal things. One of the men said his girl friend was going to have

a baby and he didn't know where he was going to get

the money to do anything about it. So one of the other men asked him why didn't he sell something. He said he didn't have anything to sell. Whereupon the third man (he was rather delicate and didn't look as if he belonged with the others) said yes, there was something he could sell: *dreams*. Even I laughed, but the man shook his head and said very seriously: no, it was perfectly true, his wife's aunt, Miss Mozart, worked for a rich man who bought dreams, regular night-time dreams – from anybody. And he wrote down the man's name and address and gave it to his friend; but the man simply left it lying on the table. It was too crazy for him, he said.'

'Me, too,' Estelle put in a little righteously.

'I don't know,' said Sylvia, lighting a cigarette. 'But I couldn't get it out of my head. The name written on the paper was A. F. Revercomb and the address was on East Seventy-eighth Street. I only glanced at it for a moment, but it was ... I don't know, I couldn't seem to forget it. It was beginning to give me a headache. So I left the office early ...'

Slowly and with emphasis, Estelle put down her coffee cup. 'Honey, listen, you don't mean you went to see him, this Revercomb nut?'

7

'I didn't mean to,' she said, immediately embarrassed. To try and tell about it she now realized was a mistake. Estelle had no imagination, she would never understand. So her eyes narrowed, the way they always did when she composed a lie. 'And, as a matter of fact, I didn't,' she said flatly. 'I started to; but then I realized how silly it was, and went for a walk instead.'

'That was sensible of you,' said Estelle as she began stacking dishes in the kitchen sink. 'Imagine what might have happened. Buying dreams! Whoever heard! Uh uh, honey, this sure isn't Easton.'

Before retiring, Sylvia took a seconal, something she seldom did; but she knew otherwise she would never rest, not with her mind so nimble and somersaulting; then, too, she felt a curious sadness, a sense of loss, as though she'd been the victim of some real or even moral theft, as though, in fact, the boys encountered in the park had snatched (abruptly she switched on the light) her purse. The envelope Miss Mozart had handed her: it was in the purse, and until now she had forgotten it. She tore it open. Inside there was a blue note folded around a bill; on the note there was written: *In payment of one dream*, 8 $5. And now she believed it; it was true, and she had sold Mr Revercomb a dream. Could it be really so simple as that? She laughed a little as she turned off the light again. If she were to sell a dream only twice a week, think of what she could do: a place somewhere all her own, she thought, deepening towards sleep; ease, like firelight, wavered over her, and there came the moment of twilit lantern slides, deeply deeper. His lips, his arms: telescoped, descending; and distastefully she kicked away the blanket. Were these cold man-arms the arms Estelle had spoken of? Mr Revercomb's lips brushed her ear as he leaned far into her sleep. Tell me? he whispered.

It was a week before she saw him again, a Sunday afternoon in early December. She'd left the apartment intending to see a movie, but somehow, and as though it had happened without her knowledge, she found herself on Madison Avenue, two blocks from Mr Revercomb's. It was a cold, silver-skied day, with winds sharp and catching as hollyhock; in store windows icicles of Christmas tinsel twinkled amid mounds of sequined snow: all to Sylvia's distress, for she hated holidays, those times when one is most alone. In one window she saw a spectacle which made her stop still. It was a life-sized, mechanical Santa Claus; slapping his stomach he rocked back and forth in a frenzy of electrical mirth. You could hear beyond the thick glass his squeaky uproarious laughter. The longer she watched the more evil he seemed, until, finally, with a shudder, she turned and made her way into the street of Mr Revercomb's house. It was, from the outside, an ordinary town house, perhaps a trifle less polished, less imposing than some others, but relatively grand all the same. Winter-withered ivy writhed about the leaded window-panes and trailed in octopus ropes over the door; at the sides of the door were two small stone lions with blind, chipped eyes. Sylvia took a breath, then rang the bell. Mr Revercomb's pale and charming Negro recognized her with a courteous smile.

On the previous visit, the parlour in which she had awaited her audience with Mr Revercomb had been empty except for herself. This time there were others present, women of several appearances, and an excessively nervous, gnat-eyed young man. Had this group been what it resembled, namely, patients in a doctor's anteroom, he would have seemed either an expectant father or a victim of St Vitus. Sylvia was seated next to him, and his fidgety eyes unbuttoned her rapidly: whatever he saw apparently intrigued him very little, and Sylvia was grateful when he went back to his twitchy preoccupations. Gradually, though, she became conscious of how interested in her the assemblage seemed; in the dim, doubtful light of the plant-filled room their gazes were more rigid than the chairs upon which they sat; one woman was particularly restless. Ordinarily, her face would have had a soft commonplace sweetness, but now, watching Sylvia, it was ugly with distrust, jealousy. As though trying to tame some creature which might suddenly spring full-fanged, she sat stroking a flea-bitten neck fur, her stare continuing its assault until the earthquake footstep of Miss Mozart was heard in the hall. Immediately, and like frightened students, the group, separating into their individual identities, came to attention. 'You, Mr Pocker,' accused Miss Mozart, 'you're next!' and Mr Pocker, wringing his hands, jittering his eyes, followed after her. In the dusk-room the gathering settled again like sun motes.

It began then to rain; melting window reflections quivered on the walls, and Mr Revercomb's young butler, seeping through the room, stirred a fire in the grate, set tea things upon a table. Sylvia, nearest the fire, felt drowsy with warmth and the noise of rain; her head tilted sideways, she closed her eyes, neither asleep nor really awake. For a long while only the   11 crystal swingings of a clock scratched the polished silence of Mr Revercomb's house. And then, abruptly, there was an enormous commotion in the hall, capsizing the room into a fury of sound: a bull-deep voice, vulgar as red, roared out: 'Stop Oreilly? The ballet butler and who else?' The owner of this voice, a tub-shaped, brick-coloured little man, shoved his way to the parlour threshold, where he stood drunkenly see-sawing from foot to foot. 'Well, well, well,' he said, his gin-hoarse voice descending on the scale, 'and all these ladies before me? But Oreilly is a gentleman, Oreilly waits his turn.'

'Not here, he doesn't,' said Miss Mozart, stealing up behind him and seizing him sternly by the collar. His face went even redder and his eyes bubbled out: 'You're choking me,' he gasped, but Miss Mozart, whose green-pale hands were as strong as oak roots, jerked his tie still tighter, and propelled him towards the door, which presently slammed with shattering effect: a tea cup tinkled, and dry dahlia leaves tumbled from their heights. The lady with the fur slipped an aspirin into her mouth. 'Disgusting,' she said, and the others, all except Sylvia, laughed delicately, admiringly, as Miss Mozart strode past dusting her hands.

12   It was raining thick and darkly when Sylvia left

Mr Revercomb's. She looked around the desolate street for a taxi; there was nothing, however, and no one; yes, someone, the drunk man who had caused the disturbance. Like a lonely city child, he was leaning against a parked car and bouncing a rubber ball up and down. 'Lookit, kid,' he said to Sylvia, 'lookit, I just found this ball. Do you suppose that means good luck?' Sylvia smiled at him; for all his bravado, she thought him rather harmless, and there was a quality in his face, some grinning sadness suggesting a clown minus make-up. Juggling his ball, he skipped along after her as she headed toward Madison Avenue. 'I'll bet I made a fool of myself in there,' he said. 'When I do things like that I just want to sit down and cry.' Standing so long in the rain seemed to have sobered him considerably. 'But she ought not to have choked me that way; damn, she's too rough. I've known some rough women: my sister Berenice could brand the wildest bull; but that other one, she's the roughest of the lot. Mark Oreilly's word, she's going to end up in the electric chair,' he said, and smacked his lips. 'They've got no cause to treat me like that. It's every bit his fault anyhow. I didn't have an awful lot to begin with, but then he took it every bit, and now I've got *niente*, kid, *niente*.' 13

'That's too bad,' said Sylvia, though she did not know what she was being sympathetic about. 'Are you a clown, Mr Oreilly?'

'Was,' he said.

By this time they had reached the avenue, but Sylvia did not even look for a taxi; she wanted to walk on in the rain with the man who had been a clown. 'When I was a little girl I only liked clown dolls,' she told him. 'My room at home was like a circus.'

'I've been other things besides a clown. I have sold insurance, too.'

'Oh?' said Sylvia, disappointed. 'And what do you do now?'

Oreilly chuckled and threw his ball especially high; after the catch his head still remained tilted upward. 'I watch the sky,' he said. 'There I am with my suitcase travelling through the blue. It's where you travel when you've got no place else to go. But what do I do on this planet? I have stolen, begged, and sold my dreams – all for purposes of whiskey. A man cannot travel in the blue without a bottle. Which brings us to a point: how'd you take it, baby, if I asked for the loan of a dollar?'

'I'd take it fine,' Sylvia replied, and paused, uncertain of what she'd say next. They wandered along so slowly, the stiff rain enclosing them like an insulating pressure; it was as though she were walking with a childhood doll, one grown miraculous and capable; she reached and held his hand: dear clown travelling in the blue. 'But I haven't got a dollar. All I've got is seventy cents.'

'No hard feelings,' said Oreilly. 'But honest, is that the kind of money he's paying nowadays?'

Sylvia knew whom he meant. 'No, no – as a matter of fact, I didn't sell him a dream.' She made to attempt to explain; she didn't understand it herself. Confronting the greying invisibility of Mr Revercomb (impeccable, exact as a scale, surrounded in a cologne of clinical odours; flat grey eyes planted like seed in the anonymity of his face and sealed within steel-dull lenses), she could not remember a dream, and so she told of two thieves who had chased her through the park and in and out among the swings of a playground. 'Stop, he said for me to stop; there are dreams and dreams, he said, but that is not a real one, that is one you are making up. Now how do you suppose he knew that? So I told him another dream; it was about him, of how he held me in the night with balloons rising and moons falling all around. He said he was not interested in dreams concerning himself.' Miss Mozart, who transcribed the dreams in shorthand, was told to call the next person. 'I don't think I will go back there again,' she said.

'You will,' said Oreilly. 'Look at me, even I go back, and he has long since finished with me, Master Misery.'

'Master Misery? Why do you call him that?'

They had reached the corner where the maniacal Santa Claus rocked and bellowed. His laughter echoed in the rainy squeaking street, and a shadow of him swayed in the rainbow lights of the pavement. Oreilly, turning his back upon the Santa Claus, smiled and said: 'I call him Master Misery on account of that's who he is. Master Misery. Only maybe you call him something else; anyway, he is the same fellow, and you must've known him. All mothers tell their kids about him: he lives in hollows of trees, he comes down chimneys late at night, he lurks in graveyards and you can hear his step in the attic. The sonofabitch, he is a thief and a threat: he will take everything you have and end by leaving you nothing, not even a dream. Boo!' he shouted, and laughed louder than Santa Claus. 'Now do you know
16 who he is?'

Sylvia nodded. 'I know who he is. My family called him something else. But I can't remember what. It was long ago.'

'But you remember him?'

'Yes, I remember him.'

'Then call him Master Misery,' he said, and, bouncing his ball, walked away from her. 'Mas-ter Mis-er-y . . .'

It was hard to look at Estelle, for she was in front of a window, and the window was filled with windy sun, which hurt Sylvia's eyes, and the glass rattled, which hurt her head. Also, Estelle was lecturing. Her nasal voice sounded as though her throat were a depository of rusty razor blades. 'I wish you could see yourself,' she was saying. Or was that something she'd said a long while back? Never mind. 'I don't know what's happened to you: I'll bet you don't weigh a hundred pounds, I can see every bone and vein, and your hair! You look like a poodle.'

Sylvia passed a hand over her forehead. 'What time is it, Estelle?'

'It's four,' she said, interrupting herself long enough to look at her watch. 'But where is your watch?'

'I sold it,' said Sylvia, too tired to lie. It did not matter. She had sold so many things, including her beaver coat and gold mesh evening bag.

Estelle shook her head. 'I give up, honey, I plain give up. And that was the watch your mother gave you for graduation. It's a shame,' she said, and made an old-maid noise with her mouth, 'a pity and a shame. I'll never understand why you left us. That is your business, I'm sure; only how could you have left us for this . . . this . . .?'

'Dump,' supplied Sylvia, using the word advisedly. It was a furnished room in the East Sixties between Second and Third Avenues. Large enough for a daybed and a splintery old bureau with a mirror like a cataracted eye, it had one window, which looked out on a vast vacant lot (you could hear the tough afternoon voices of desperate running boys) and in the distance, like an exclamation point for the skyline, there was the black smokestack of a factory. This smokestack occurred frequently in her dreams; it never failed to arouse Miss Mozart: 'Phallic, phallic,' she would mutter, glancing up from her shorthand. The floor of the room was a garbage pail of books begun but never finished, antique newspapers, even orange hulls, fruit cores, underwear, a spilled powder box.

Estelle kicked her way through this trash, and sat down on the daybed. 'Honey, you don't know, but I've been worried crazy. I mean I've got pride and all that and if you don't like me, well OK; but you've got no right to stay away like this and not let me hear from you in over a month. So today I said to Bootsy, Bootsy I've got a feeling something terrible has happened to Sylvia. You can imagine how I felt when I called your office and they told me you hadn't worked there for the last four weeks. What happened, were you fired?'

'Yes, I was fired.' Sylvia began to sit up. 'Please, Estelle – I've got to get ready; I've got an appointment.'

'Be still. You're not going anywhere till I know what's wrong. The landlady downstairs told me you were found sleep–walking . . .'

'What do you mean talking to her? Why are you spying on me?'

Estelle's eyes puckered, as though she were going to cry. She put her hand over Sylvia's and petted it gently. 'Tell me, honey, is it because of a man?'

'It's because of a man, yes,' said Sylvia, laughter at the edge of her voice.

'You should have come to me before,' Estelle 19

sighed. 'I know about men. That is nothing for you to be ashamed of. A man can have a way with a woman that kind of makes her forget everything else. If Henry wasn't the fine upstanding potential lawyer that he is, why, I would still love him, and do things for him that before I knew what it was like to be with a man would have seemed shocking and horrible. But, honey, this fellow you've mixed up with, he's taking advantage of you.'

'It's not that kind of relationship,' said Sylvia, getting up and locating a pair of stockings in the *furor* of her bureau drawers. 'It hasn't got anything to do with love. Forget about it. In fact, go home and forget about me altogether.'

Estelle looked at her narrowly. 'You scare me, Sylvia; you really scare me.' Sylvia laughed and went on getting dressed. 'Do you remember a long time ago when I said you ought to get married?'

'Uh huh. And now you listen.' Sylvia turned around; there was a row of hairpins spaced across her mouth; she extracted them one at a time all the while she talked. 'You talk about getting married as though it were the answer absolute; very well, up to a point I agree. Sure, I want to be loved; who the
20   hell doesn't? But even if I was willing to compromise,

where is the man I'm going to marry? Believe me, he must've fallen down a manhole. I mean it seriously when I say there are no men in New York – and even if there were, how do you meet them? Every man I ever met here who seemed the slightest bit attractive was either married, too poor to get married, or queer. And anyway, this is no place to fall in love; this is where you ought to come when you want to get over being in love. Sure, I suppose I could marry somebody; but I do not want that. Do I?'

Estelle shrugged. 'Then what do you want?'

'More than is coming to me.' She poked the last hairpin into place, and smoothed her eyebrows before the mirror. 'I have an appointment, Estelle, and it is time for you to go now.'

'I can't leave you like this,' said Estelle, her hand waving helplessly around the room. 'Sylvia, you were my childhood friend.'

'That is just the point: we're not children any more; at least, I'm not. No, I want you to go home, and I don't want you to come here again. I just want you to forget about me.'

Estelle fluttered at her eyes with a handkerchief, and by the time she reached the door she was weeping quite loudly. Sylvia could not afford remorse:

having been mean, there was nothing to be but meaner. 'Go on,' she said, following Estelle into the hall, 'and write home any damn nonsense about me you want to!' Letting out a wail that brought other roomers to their doors, Estelle fled down the stairs.

After this Sylvia went back into her room and sucked a piece of sugar to take the sour taste out of her mouth: it was her grandmother's remedy for bad tempers. Then she got down on her knees and pulled from under the bed a cigar box she kept hidden there. When you opened the box it played a home-made and somewhat disorganized version of 'Oh How I Hate to Get Up in the Morning'. Her brother had made the music-box and given it to her on her fourteenth birthday. Eating the sugar, she'd thought of her grandmother, and hearing the tune, she thought of her brother; the rooms of the house where they had lived rotated before her, all dark and she like a light moving among them: up the stairs, down, out and through, spring sweet and lilac shadows in the air and the creaking of a porch swing. All gone, she thought, calling their names, and now I am absolutely alone. The music stopped. But it went on in her head; she could hear it bugling above the child-cries of the vacant lot. And it interfered with her reading. She was reading a little diary-like book she kept inside the box. In this book she wrote down the essentials of her dreams; they were endless now, and it was so hard to remember. Today she would tell Mr Revercomb about the three blind children. He would like that. The prices he paid varied, and she was sure this was at least a ten-dollar dream. The cigar-box anthem followed her down the stairs and through the streets and she longed for it to go away.

In the store where Santa Claus had been there was a new and equally unnerving exhibit. Even when she was late to Mr Revercomb's, as now, Sylvia was compelled to pause by the window. A plaster girl with intense glass eyes sat astride a bicycle pedalling at the maddest pace; though its wheel spokes spun hypnotically, the bicycle of course never budged: all that effort and the poor girl going nowhere. It was a pitifully human situation, and one that Sylvia could so exactly identify with herself that she always felt a real pang. The music-box rewound in her head: the tune, her brother, the house, a high-school dance, the house, the tune! Couldn't Mr Revercomb hear it? His penetrating gaze carried such dull suspicion. But he seemed pleased with her dream, and, when 23 she left, Miss Mozart gave her an envelope containing ten dollars.

'I had a ten-dollar dream,' she told Oreilly, and Oreilly, rubbing his hands together, said, 'Fine! Fine! But that's just my luck, baby – you should've got here sooner 'cause I went and did a terrible thing. I walked into a liquor store up the street, snatched a quart and ran.' Sylvia didn't believe him until he produced from his pinned-together overcoat a bottle of bourbon, already half gone. 'You're going to get in trouble some day,' she said, 'and then what would happen to me? I don't know what I would do without you.' Oreilly laughed and poured a shot of the whiskey into a water glass. They were sitting in an all-night cafeteria, a great glaring food depot alive with blue mirrors and raw murals. Although to Sylvia it seemed a sordid place, they met there frequently for dinner; but even if she could have afforded it she did not know where else they could go, for together they presented a curious aspect: a young girl and a doddering, drunken man. Even here people often stared at them; if they stared long enough, Oreilly would stiffen with dignity and say: 'Hello, hot lips, I remember you from way back. Still working in the men's room?' But usually they were left to themselves, and sometimes they would sit talking until two and three in the morning.

'It's a good thing the rest of Master Misery's crowd don't know he gave you that ten bucks. One of them would say you stole the dream. I had that happen once. Eaten up, all of 'em, never saw such a bunch of sharks, worse than actors or clowns or businessmen. Crazy, if you think about it: you worry whether you're going to sleep, if you're going to have a dream, if you're going to remember the dream. Round and round. So you get a couple of bucks, so you rush to the nearest liquor store – or the nearest sleeping-pill machine. And first thing you know, you're roaming your way up outhouse alley. Why, baby, you know what it's like? It's just like life.'

'No, Oreilly, that's what it isn't like. It hasn't anything to do with life. It has more to do with being dead. I feel as though everything were being taken from me, as though some thief were stealing me down to the bone. Oreilly, I tell you I haven't an ambition, and there used to be so much. I don't understand it and I don't know what to do.'

He grinned. 'And you say it isn't like life? Who understands life and who knows what to do?'

'Be serious,' she said. 'Be serious and put away

that whiskey and eat your soup before it gets stone cold.' She lighted a cigarette, and the smoke, smarting her eyes, intensified her frown. 'If only I knew what he wanted with those dreams, all typed and filed. What does he do with them? You're right when you say he is Master Misery . . . He can't be simply some silly quack; it can't be so meaningless as that. But why does he want dreams? Help me, Oreilly, think, think: what does it mean?'

Squinting one eye, Oreilly poured himself another drink; the clownlike twist of his mouth hardened into a line of scholarly straightness. 'That is a million-dollar question, kid. Why don't you ask something easy, like how to cure the common cold? Yes, kid, what does it mean? I have thought about it a good deal. I have thought about it in the process of making love to a woman, and I have thought about it in the middle of a poker game.' He tossed a drink down his throat and shuddered. 'Now a sound can start a dream; the noise of one car passing in the night can drop a hundred sleepers into the deep parts of themselves. It's funny to think of that one car racing through the dark, trailing so many dreams. Sex, a sudden change of light, a pickle, these are the little keys that can open up our insides, too. But most dreams begin because there are furies inside of us that blow open all the doors. I don't believe in Jesus Christ, but I do believe in people's souls; and I figure it this way, baby: dreams are the mind of the soul and the secret truth about us. Now Master Misery, maybe he hasn't got a soul, so bit by bit he borrows yours, steals it like he would steal your dolls or the chicken wing off your plate. Hundreds of souls have passed through him and gone into a filing case.'

'Oreilly, be serious,' she said again, annoyed because she thought he was making more jokes. 'And look, your soup is . . .' She stopped abruptly, startled by Oreilly's peculiar expression. He was looking toward the entrance. Three men were there, two policemen and a civilian wearing a clerk's cloth jacket. The clerk was pointing toward their table. Oreilly's eyes circled the room with trapped despair; he sighed then, and leaned back in his seat, ostentatiously pouring himself another drink. 'Good evening, gentlemen,' he said, when the official party confronted him, 'will you join us for a drink?'

'You can't arrest him,' cried Sylvia, 'you can't arrest a clown!' She threw her ten-dollar bill at them, but the policemen did not pay any attention, and she began to pound the table. All the customers in the place were staring, and the manager came running up, wringing his hands. The police said for Oreilly to get to his feet. 'Certainly,' Oreilly said, 'though I do think it shocking you have to trouble yourselves with such petty crimes as mine when everywhere there are master thieves afoot. For instance, this pretty child,' he stepped between the officers and pointed to Sylvia, 'she is the recent victim of a major theft: poor baby, she has had her soul stolen.'

For two days following Oreilly's arrest, Sylvia did not leave her room: sun on the window, then dark. By the third day she had run out of cigarettes, so she ventured as far as the corner delicatessen. She bought a package of cupcakes, a can of sardines, a newspaper and cigarettes. In all this time she'd not eaten and it was a light, delicious, sharpening sensation; but the climb back up the stairs, the relief of closing the door, these so exhausted her she could not quite make the daybed. She slid down to the floor and did not move until it was day again. She thought afterwards that she'd been there about twenty minutes.

28 Turning on the radio as loud as it would go, she

dragged a chair up to the window and opened the newspaper on her lap: *Lana Denies, Russia Rejects, Miners Conciliate*: of all things this was the saddest, that life goes on: if one leaves one's lover, life should stop for him, and if one disappears from the world, then the world should stop, too; and it never did. And that was the real reason for most people getting up in the morning: not because it would matter but because it wouldn't. But if Mr Revercomb succeeded finally in collecting all the dreams out of every head, perhaps – the idea slipped, became entangled with radio and newspaper. *Falling Temperatures*. A snow-storm moving across Colorado, across the West, fall-ing upon all the small towns, yellowing every light, filling every footfall, falling now and here; but how quickly it had come, the snowstorm: the roofs, the vacant lot, the distance deep in white and deepening, like sheep. She looked at the paper and she looked at the snow. But it must have been snowing all day. It could not have just started. There was no sound of traffic; in the swirling wastes of the vacant lot chil-dren circled a bonfire; a car, buried at the kerb, winked its headlights: help, help! silent, like the heart's distress. She crumbled a cupcake and sprink-led it on the windowsill: north-birds would come to 29 keep her company. And she left the window open for them; snow-wind scattered flakes that dissolved on the floor like April-fool jewels. *Presents Life Can be Beautiful*: turn down that radio! The witch of the woods was tapping at her door: Yes, Mrs Halloran, she said, and turned off the radio altogether. Snow-quiet, sleep-silent, only the fun-fire faraway songsinging of children; and the room was blue with cold, colder than the cold of fairytales: lie down my heart among the igloo flowers of snow. Mr Revercomb, why do you wait upon the threshold? Ah, do come inside, it is so cold out there.

But her moment of waking was warm and held. The window was closed, and a man's arms were around her. He was singing to her, his voice gentle but jaunty: *cherryberry, moneyberry, happyberry pie, but the best old pie is a loveberry pie* . . .

'Oreilly, is it — is it really you?'

He squeezed her. 'Baby's awake now. And how does she feel?'

'I had thought I was dead,' she said, and happiness winged around inside her like a bird lamed but still flying. She tried to hug him and she was too weak. 'I love you, Oreilly; you are my only friend and I was so frightened. I thought I would never see you again.' She paused, remembering. 'But why aren't you in jail?'

Oreilly's face got all tickled and pink. 'I never was in jail,' he said mysteriously. 'But first, let's have something to eat. I brought some things up from the delicatessen this morning.'

She had a sudden feeling of floating. 'How long have you been here?'

'Since yesterday,' he said, fussing around with bundles and paper plates. 'You let me in yourself.'

'That's impossible. I don't remember it at all.'

'I know,' he said, leaving it at that. 'Here, drink your milk like a good kid and I'll tell you a real wicked story. Oh, it's wild,' he promised, slapping his sides gladly and looking more than ever like a clown. 'Well, like I said, I never was in jail and this bit of fortune came to me because there I was being hustled down the street by those bindlestiffs when who should I see come swinging along but the gorilla woman: you guessed it, Miss Mozart. Hi, I says to her, off to the barber shop for a shave? It's about time you were put under arrest, she says, and smiles at one of the cops. Do your duty, officer. Oh, I says to her, I'm not under arrest. Me, I'm just on my way to the station house to give them the lowdown on 31 you, you dirty communist. You can imagine what sort of holler she set up then; she grabbed hold of me and the cops grabbed hold of her. Can't say I didn't warn them: careful, boys, I said, she's got hair on her chest. And she sure did lay about her. So I just sort of walked off down the street. Never have believed in standing around watching fist-fights the way people do in this city.'

Oreilly stayed with her in the room over the weekend. It was like the most beautiful party Sylvia could remember; she'd never laughed so much, for one thing, and no one, certainly no one in her family, had ever made her feel so loved. Oreilly was a fine cook, and he fixed delicious dishes on the little electric stove; once he scooped snow off the window-sill and made sherbet flavoured with strawberry syrup. By Sunday she was strong enough to dance. They turned on the radio and she danced until she fell to her knees, windless and laughing. 'I'll never be afraid again,' she said. 'I hardly know what I was afraid of to begin with.'

'The same things you'll be afraid of the next time,' Oreilly told her quietly. 'That is a quality of Master Misery: no one ever knows what he is – not even children, and they know mostly everything.'

Sylvia went to the window; an arctic whiteness lay over the city, but the snow had stopped, and the night sky was as clear as ice: there, riding above the river, she saw the first star of evening. 'I see the first star,' she said, crossing her fingers.

'And what do you wish when you see the first star?'

'I wish to see another star,' she said. 'At least that is what I usually wish.'

'But tonight?'

She sat down on the floor and leaned her head against his knee. 'Tonight I wished that I could have back my dreams.'

'Don't we all?' Oreilly said, stroking her hair. 'But then what would you do? I mean what would you do if you could have them back?'

Sylvia was silent a moment; when she spoke her eyes were gravely distant. 'I would go home,' she said slowly. 'And that is a terrible decision, for it would mean giving up most of my other dreams. But if Mr Revercomb would let me have them back, then I would go home tomorrow.'

Saying nothing, Oreilly went to the closet and brought back her coat. 'But why?' she asked as he helped her on with it. 'Never mind,' he said, 'just do

33

what I tell you. We're going to pay Mr Revercomb a call, and you're going to ask him to give you back your dreams. It's a chance.'

Sylvia balked at the door. 'Please, Oreilly, don't make me go. I can't, please, I'm afraid.'

'I thought you said you'd never be afraid again.'

But once in the street he hurried her so quickly against the wind she did not have time to be frightened. It was Sunday, stores were closed and the traffic lights seemed to wink only for them, for there were no moving cars along the snow-deep avenue. Sylvia even forgot where they were going, and chattered of trivial oddments: right here at this corner is where she'd seen Garbo, and over there, that is where the old woman was run over. Presently, however, she stopped, out of breath and overwhelmed with sudden realization. 'I can't, Oreilly,' she said, pulling back. 'What can I say to him?'

'Make it like a business deal,' said Oreilly. 'Tell him straight out that you want your dreams, and if he'll give them to you you'll pay back all the money: on the instalment plan, naturally. It's simple enough, kid. Why the hell couldn't he give them back? They are all right there in a filing case.'

34   This speech was somehow convincing and, stamp-

ing her frozen feet, Sylvia went ahead with a certain courage. 'That's the kid,' he said. They separated on Third Avenue, Oreilly being of the opinion that Mr Revercomb's immediate neighbourhood was not for the moment precisely safe. He confined himself in a doorway, now and then lighting a match and singing aloud: *but the best old pie is a whiskeyberry pie*! Like a wolf, a long thin dog came padding over the moon-slats under the elevated, and across the street there were the misty shapes of men ganged around a bar: the idea of maybe cadging a drink in there made him groggy.

Just as he had decided on perhaps trying something of the sort, Sylvia appeared. And she was in his arms before he knew that it was really her. 'It can't be so bad, sweetheart,' he said softly, holding her as best he could. 'Don't cry, baby; it's too cold to cry: you'll chap your face.' As she strangled for words, her crying evolved into a tremulous, unnatural laugh. The air was filled with the smoke of her laughter. 'Do you know what he said?' she gasped. 'Do you know what he said when I asked for my dreams?' Her head fell back, and her laughter rose and carried over the street like an abandoned, wildly coloured kite. Oreilly had finally to shake her by the 35 shoulders. 'He said – I couldn't have them back because – because he'd used them all up.'

She was silent then, her face smoothing into an expressionless calm. She put her arm through Oreilly's, and together they moved down the street; but it was as if they were friends pacing a platform, each waiting for the other's train, and when they reached the corner he cleared his throat and said: 'I guess I'd better turn off here. It's as likely a spot as any.'

Sylvia held on to his sleeve. 'But where will you go, Oreilly?'

'Travelling in the blue,' he said, trying a smile that didn't work out very well.

She opened her purse. 'A man cannot travel in the blue without a bottle,' she said, and kissing him on the cheek, slipped five dollars in his pocket.

'Bless you, baby.'

It did not matter that it was the last of her money, that now she would have to walk home, and alone. The pilings of snow were like the white waves of a white sea, and she rode upon them, carried by winds and tides of the moon. I do not know what I want, and perhaps I shall never know, but my only wish from every star will always be another star; and truly I am not afraid, she thought. Two boys came out of a bar and stared at her; in some park some long time ago she'd seen two boys and they might be the same. Truly I am not afraid, she thought, hearing their snowy footsteps following her; and anyway, there was nothing left to steal.

Overheard in a cowboy bar in Roswell, New Mexico . . .

FIRST COWBOY: Hey, Jed. How are you? How you feeling?

SECOND COWBOY: Good! Real good. I feel so good I didn't have to jack off this morning to get my heart started.

'*Carissimo!*' she cried. 'You're just what I'm looking for. A lunch date. The duchess stood me up.'

'Black or white?' I said.

'White,' she said, reversing my direction on the sidewalk.

White is Wallis Windsor, whereas the Black Duchess is what her friends call Perla Apfeldorf, the Brazilian wife of a notoriously racist South African diamond industrialist. As for the lady who also knew the distinction, she was indeed a lady – Lady Ina Coolbirth, an American married to a British chemicals tycoon and a lot of woman in every way. Tall, taller than most men, Ina was a big breezy peppy broad, born and raised on a ranch in Montana.

'This is the second time she's canceled,' Ina Coolbirth continued. 'She says she has hives. Or the duke has hives. One or the other. Anyway, I've still got a table at Côte Basque. So, shall we? Because I do need someone to talk to, really. And, thank God, Jonesy, it can be you.'

Côte Basque is on East Fifty-fifth Street, directly across from the St Regis. It was the site of the original Le Pavillon, founded in 1940 by the honorable restaurateur Henri Soulé. M. Soulé abandoned the premises because of a feud with his landlord, the late president of Columbia Pictures, a sleazy Hollywood hood named Harry Cohn (who, upon learning that Sammy Davis, Jr, was 'dating' his blonde star Kim Novak, ordered a hit man to call Davis and tell him: 'Listen, Sambo, you're already missing one eye. How'd you like to try for none?' The next day Davis married a Las Vegas chorus girl – colored). Like Côte Basque, the original Pavillon consisted of a small entrance area, a bar to the left of this, and in the rear, through an archway, a large red-plush dining room. The bar and main room formed an

Outer Hebrides, an Elba to which Soulé exiled second-class patrons. Preferred clients, selected by the proprietor with unerring *snobisme*, were placed in the banquette-lined entrance area – a practice pursued by every New York restaurant of established chic: Lafayette, The Colony, La Grenouille, La Caravelle. These tables, always nearest the door, are drafty, afford the least privacy, but nevertheless, to be seated at one, or not, is a status-sensitive citizen's moment of truth. Harry Cohn never made it at Pavillon. It didn't matter that he was a hotshot Hollywood hottentot or even that he was Soulé's landlord. Soulé saw him for the shoulder-padded counter-jumper Cohn was and accordingly ushered him to a table in the sub-zero regions of the rear room. Cohn cursed, he huffed, puffed, revenged himself by upping and upping the restaurant's rent. So Soulé simply moved to more regal quarters in the Ritz Tower. However, while Soulé was still settling there, Harry Cohn cooled (Jerry Wald, when asked why he attended the funeral, replied: 'Just to be sure the bastard was dead'), and Soulé, nostalgic for his old stamping ground, again leased the address from the new custodians and created, as a second enterprise, a sort of boutique variation on Le Pavillon: La Côte Basque.

Lady Ina, of course, was allotted an impeccable position – the fourth table on the left as you enter. She was escorted to it by none other than M. Soulé, distrait as ever, pink and glazed as a marzipan pig.

'Lady Coolbirth . . . ,' he muttered, his perfectionist eyes spinning about in search of cankered roses and awkward waiters. 'Lady Coolbirth . . . umn . . . very nice . . . umn . . . and Lord Coolbirth? . . . umn . . . today we have on the wagon a very nice saddle of lamb . . .'

She consulted me, a glance, and said: 'I think not anything off the wagon. It arrives too quickly. Let's have something that takes forever. So that we can get drunk and disorderly. Say a soufflé Furstenberg. Could you do that, Monsieur Soulé?'

He tutted his tongue – on two counts: he disapproves of customers dulling their taste buds with alcohol, and also: 'Furstenberg is a great nuisance. An uproar.'

Delicious, though: a froth of cheese and spinach into which an assortment of poached eggs has been sunk strategically, so that, when struck by your fork, the soufflé is moistened with golden rivers of egg yolk.

'An uproar,' said Ina, 'is exactly what I want,' and

the proprietor, touching his sweat-littered forehead with a bit of handkerchief, acquiesced.

Then she decided against cocktails, saying: 'Why not have a proper reunion?' From the wine steward she ordered a bottle of Roederer's Cristal. Even for those who dislike champagne, myself among them, there are two champagnes one can't refuse: Dom Pérignon and the even superior Cristal, which is bottled in a natural-colored glass that displays its pale blaze, a chilled fire of such prickly dryness that, swallowed, seems not to have been swallowed at all, but instead to have turned to vapors on the tongue and burned there to one damp sweet ash.

'Of course,' said Ina, 'champagne does have one serious drawback: swilled as a regular thing, a certain sourness settles in the tummy, and the result is permanent bad breath. Really incurable. Remember Arturo's breath, bless his heart? And Cole adored champagne. God, I do miss Cole so, dotty as he was those last years. Did I ever tell you the story about Cole and the stud wine steward? I can't remember quite where he worked. He was Italian, so it couldn't have been here or Pav. The Colony? Odd: I see him clearly — a nut-brown man, beautifully flat, with oiled hair and the sexiest jawline — but I can't see *where* I see him. He was a southern Italian, so they called him Dixie, and Teddie Whitestone got knocked up by him – Bill Whitestone aborted her himself under the impression it was his doing. And perhaps it was – in quite another context – but still I think it rather dowdy, unnatural, if you will, a doctor aborting his own wife. Teddie Whitestone wasn't alone; there was a queue of gals greasing Dixie's palm with billets-doux. Cole's approach was creative: he invited Dixie to his apartment under the pretext of getting advice on the laying in of a new wine cellar – Cole! who knew more about wine than that dago ever dreamed. So they were sitting there on the couch – the lovely suede one Billy Baldwin made for Cole – all very informal, and Cole kisses this fellow on the cheek, and Dixie grins and says: "That will cost you five hundred dollars, Mr Porter." Cole just laughs and squeezes Dixie's leg. "Now that will cost you a thousand dollars, Mr Porter." Then Cole realized this piece of pizza was serious; and so he unzippered him, hauled it out, shook it, and said: "What will be the full price on the use of that?" Dixie told him two thousand dollars. Cole went straight to his desk, wrote a check and handed it to him. And he said: 43

"Miss Otis regrets she's unable to lunch today. Now get out.'"

The Cristal was being poured. Ina tasted it. 'It's not cold enough. But ahhh!' She swallowed again. 'I do miss Cole. And Howard Sturgis. Even Papa; after all, he did write about me in *Green Hills of Africa*. And Uncle Willie. Last week in London I went to a party at Drue Heinz's and got stuck with Princess Margaret. Her mother's a darling, but the rest of that family! – though Prince Charles may amount to something. But basically, royals think there are just three categories: colored folk, white folk, and royals. Well, I was about to doze off, she's such a drone, when suddenly she announced, apropos of nothing, that she had decided she really didn't like "poufs"! An extraordinary remark, source considered. Remember the joke about who got the first sailor? But I simply lowered my eyes, *très* Jane Austen, and said: "In that event, ma'am, I fear you will spend a very lonely old age." Her expression! – I thought she might turn me into a pumpkin.'

There was an uncharacteristic bite and leap to Ina's voice, as though she were speeding along 44 helter-skelter to avoid confiding what it was she

wanted, but didn't want, to confide. My eyes and
ears were drifting elsewhere. The occupants of a
table placed catty-corner to ours were two people
I'd met together in Southampton last summer,
though the meeting was not of such import that I
expected them to recognize me – Gloria Vanderbilt
di Cicco Stokowski Lumet Cooper and her childhood
chum Carol Marcus Saroyan Saroyan (she married
him twice) Matthau: women in their late thirties, but
looking not much removed from those deb days
when they were grabbing Lucky Balloons at the
Stork Club.

'But what can you say,' inquired Mrs Matthau of
Mrs Cooper, 'to someone who's lost a good lover,
weighs two hundred pounds, and is in the dead
center of a nervous collapse? I don't think she's been
out of bed for a month. Or changed the sheets.
"Maureen" – this is what I *did* tell her – "Maureen,
I've been in a lot worse condition than you. I remember once when I was going around stealing sleeping
pills out of other people's medicine cabinets, saving
up to bump myself off. I was in debt up to here,
every penny I had was borrowed . . ."'

'*Dar*ling,' Mrs Cooper protested with a tiny stam-
mer, 'why didn't you come to *me*?'

'Because you're rich. It's much less difficult to borrow from the poor.'

'But, *dar*ling . . .'

Mrs Matthau proceeded. 'So I said: "Do you know what I did, Maureen? Broke as I was, I went out and hired myself a *personal* maid. My fortunes rose, my outlook changed completely, I felt loved and pampered. So if I were you, Maureen, I'd go into hock and hire some very expensive creature to run my bath and turn down the bed." Incidentally, did you go to the Logans' party?'

'For an hour.'

'How was it?'

'Marvelous. If you've never been to a party before.'

'I wanted to go. But you know Walter. I never imagined I'd marry an actor. Well, *marry* perhaps. But not for love. Yet here I've been stuck with Walter all these years and it still makes me curdle if I see his eye stray a fraction. Have you seen this new Swedish cunt called Karen something?'

'Wasn't she in some spy picture?'

'Exactly. Lovely face. Divine photographed from the bazooms up. But the legs are stricly redwood forest. Absolute tree trunks. Anyway, we met her at the Widmarks' and she was moving her eyes around and making all these little noises for Walter's benefit, and I stood it as long as I could, but when I heard Walter say, "How old are you, Karen?" I said, "For God's sake, Walter, why don't you chop off her legs and read the rings?"'

'Carol! You didn't.'

'You know you can always count on me.'

'And she heard you?'

'It wouldn't have been very interesting if she hadn't.'

Mrs Matthau extracted a comb from her purse and began drawing it through her long albino hair: another leftover from her World War II debutante nights – an era when she and all her *compères*, Gloria and Honeychile and Oona and Jinx, slouched against El Morocco upholstery ceaselessly raking their Veronica Lake locks.

'I had a letter from Oona this morning,' Mrs Matthau said.

'So did I,' Mrs Cooper said.

'Then you know they're having another baby.'

'Well, I assumed so. I always do.'

'That Charlie is a lucky bastard,' said Mrs Matthau.

'Of course, Oona would have made any man a great wife.'

'Nonsense. With Oona, only geniuses need apply. Before she met Charlie, she wanted to marry Orson Welles . . . and she wasn't even seventeen. It was Orson who introduced her to Charlie; he said: "I know just the guy for you. He's rich, he's a genius, and there's nothing that he likes more than a dutiful young daughter!"'

Mrs Cooper was thoughtful. 'If Oona hadn't married Charlie, I don't suppose I would have married Leopold.'

'And if Oona hadn't married Charlie, and you hadn't married Leopold, I wouldn't have married Bill Saroyan. Twice yet.'

The two women laughed together, their laughter like a naughty but delightfully sung duet. Though they were not physically similar – Mrs Matthau being blonder than Harlow and as lushly white as a gardenia, while the other had brandy eyes and a dark dimpled brilliance markedly present when her negroid lips flashed smiles – one sensed they were two of a kind: charmingly imcompetent adventuresses.

Mrs Matthau said: 'Remember the Salinger thing?'

'Salinger?'

'*A Perfect Day for Banana Fish.* That Salinger.'

'*Franny and Zooey.*'

'Umn-huh. You don't remember about him?'

Mrs Cooper pondered, pouted; no, she didn't.

'It was while we were still at Brearley,' said Mrs Matthau. 'Before Oona met Orson. She had a mysterious beau, this Jewish boy with a Park Avenue mother, Jerry Salinger. He wanted to be a writer, and he wrote Oona letters ten pages long while he was overseas in the army. Sort of love-letter essays, very tender, tenderer than God. Which is a bit too tender. Oona used to read them to me, and when she asked what I thought, I said it seemed to me he must be a boy who cries very easily; but what she wanted to know was whether I thought he was brilliant and talented or really just silly, and I said both, he's both, and years later when I read *Catcher in the Rye* and realized the author was Oona's Jerry, I was still inclined to that opinion.'

'I never heard a strange story about Salinger,' Mrs Cooper confided.

'I've never heard anything about him that wasn't strange. He's certainly not your normal everyday Jewish boy from Park Avenue.'

'Well, it isn't really about *him*, but about a friend of his who went to visit him in New Hampshire. He does live there, doesn't he? On some very remote farm? Well, it was February and terribly cold. One morning Salinger's friend was missing. He wasn't in his bedroom or anywhere around the house. They found him finally, deep in a snowy woods. He was lying in the snow wrapped in a blanket and holding an empty whiskey bottle. He'd killed himself by drinking the whiskey until he'd fallen asleep and frozen to death.'

After a while Mrs Matthau said: 'That *is* a strange story. It must have been lovely, though – all warm with whiskey, drifting off into the cold starry air. Why did he do it?'

'All I know is what I told you,' Mrs Cooper said.

An exiting customer, a florid-at-the-edges swarthy balding Charlie sort of fellow, stopped at their table. He fixed on Mrs Cooper a gaze that was intrigued, amused and . . . a trifle grim. He said: 'Hello, Gloria'; and she smiled: 'Hello, darling'; but her eyelids twitched as she attempted to identify him; and then he said: 'Hello, Carol. How are ya, doll?' and she knew who he was all right: 'Hello, darling. Still living in Spain?' He nodded; his glance returned to

Mrs Cooper: 'Gloria, you're as beautiful as ever. More beautiful. See ya . . .' He waved and walked away.

Mrs Cooper stared after him, scowling.

Eventually Mrs Matthau said: 'You didn't recognize him, did you?'

'N-n-no.'

'Life. Life. Really, it's too sad. There was nothing familiar about him at all?'

'Long ago. Something. A dream.'

'It wasn't a dream.'

'Carol. Stop that. Who is he?'

'Once upon a time you thought very highly of him. You cooked his meals and washed his socks' – Mrs Cooper's eyes enlarged, shifted – 'and when he was in the army you followed him from camp to camp, living in dreary furnished rooms –'

'No!'

'Yes!'

'No!'

'Yes, Gloria. Your first husband.'

'That . . . man . . . was . . . Pat di Cicco?'

'Oh, darling. Let's not brood. After all, you haven't seen him in almost twenty years. You were only a child. Isn't that,' said Mrs Matthau, offering a diversion, 'Jackie Kennedy?'

And I heard Lady Ina on the subject, too: 'I'm almost blind with these specs, but just coming in there, isn't that Mrs Kennedy? And her sister?'

It was; I knew the sister because she had gone to school with Kate McCloud, and when Kate and I were on Abner Dustin's yacht at the Feria in Seville she had lunched with us, then afterward we'd gone water-skiing together, and I've often thought of it, how perfect she was, a gleaming gold-brown girl in a white bathing suit, her white skis hissing smoothly, her brown-gold hair whipping as she swooped and skidded between the waves. So it was pleasant when she stopped to greet Lady Ina ('Did you know I was on the plane with you from London? But you were sleeping so nicely I didn't dare speak') and seeing me, remembered me: 'Why, hello there, Jonesy,' she said, her rough whispery warm voice very slightly vibrating her, 'how's your sunburn? Remember, I warned you, but you wouldn't listen.' Her laughter trailed off as she folded herself onto a banquette beside her sister, their heads inclining toward each other in whispering Bouvier conspiracy. It was puzzling how much they resembled one another without

sharing any common feature beyond identical voices

and wide-apart eyes and certain gestures, particularly a habit of staring deeply into an interlocutor's eyes while ceaselessly nodding the head with a mesmerizingly solemn sympathy.

Lady Ina observed: 'You can see those girls have swung a few big deals in their time. I know many people can't abide either of them, usually women, and I can understand that, because they don't like women and almost never have anything good to say about *any* woman. But they're perfect with men, a pair of Western geisha girls; they know how to keep a man's secrets and how to make him feel important. If I were a man, I'd fall for Lee myself. She's marvelously made, like a Tanagra figurine; she's feminine without being effeminate; and she's one of the few people I've known who can be both candid and cozy – ordinarily one cancels the other. Jackie – no, not on the same planet. Very photogenic, of course; but the effect is a little ... unrefined, exaggerated.'

I thought of an evening when I'd gone with Kate McCloud and a gang to a drag-queen contest held in a Harlem ballroom: hundreds of young queens sashaying in hand-sewn gowns to the funky honking of saxophones: Brooklyn supermarket clerks, Wall

Street runners, black dishwashers, and Puerto Rican waiters adrift in silk and fantasy, chorus boys and bank cashiers and Irish elevator boys got up as Marilyn Monroe, as Audrey Hepburn, as Jackie Kennedy. Indeed, Mrs Kennedy was the most popular inspiration; a dozen boys, the winner among them, wore her high-rise hairdo, winged eyebrows, sulky, palely painted mouth. And, in life, that is how she struck me – not as a bona fide woman, but as an artful female impersonator impersonating Mrs Kennedy.

I explained what I was thinking to Ina, and she said: 'That's what I meant by ... exaggerated.' Then: 'Did you ever know Rosita Winston? Nice woman. Half Cherokee, I believe. She had a stroke some years ago, and now she can't speak. Or, rather, she can say just one word. That very often happens after a stroke, one's left with one word out of all the words one has known. Rosita's word is "beautiful". Very appropriate, since Rosita has always loved beautiful things. What reminded me of it was old Joe Kennedy. He, too, has been left with one word. And his word is: "Goddammit!"' Ina motioned the waiter to pour champagne. 'Have I ever told you about the time he assaulted me? When I was eighteen and a guest in his house, a friend of his daughter Kek ...'

Again, my eye coasted the length of the room, catching, *en passant*, a bluebearded Seventh Avenue brassière hustler trying to con a closet-queen editor from *The New York Times*; and Diana Vreeland, the pomaded, peacock-iridescent editor of *Vogue*, sharing a table with an elderly man who suggested a precious object of discreet *extravagance*, perhaps a fine grey pearl – Mainbocher; and Mrs William S. Paley lunching with her sister, Mrs John Hay Whitney. Seated near them was a pair unknown to me: a woman forty, forty-five, no beauty but very handsomely set up inside a brown Balenciaga suit with a brooch composed of cinnamon-colored diamonds fixed to the lapel. Her companion was much younger, twenty, twenty-two, a hearty sun-browned statue who looked as if he might have spent the summer sailing alone across the Atlantic. Her son? But no, because . . . he lit a cigarette and passed it to her and their fingers touched significantly; then they were holding hands.

'. . . the old bugger slipped into my bedroom. It was about six o'clock in the morning, the ideal hour if you want to catch someone really slugged out, really by complete surprise, and when I woke up he was already between the sheets with one hand over my mouth and the other all over the place. The sheer ballsy gall of it – right there in his own house with the whole family sleeping all around us. But all those Kennedy men are the same; they're like dogs, they have to pee on every fire hydrant. Still, you had to give the old guy credit, and when he saw I wasn't going to scream he was *so* grateful . . .'

But they were not conversing, the older woman and the young seafarer; they held hands; and then he smiled and presently she smiled, too.

'Afterwards – can you imagine? – he pretended nothing had happened, there was never a wink or a nod, just the good old daddy of my schoolgirl chum. It was uncanny and rather cruel; after all, he'd had me and I'd even pretended to enjoy it: there should have been some sentimental acknowledgement, a bauble, a cigarette box . . .' She sensed my other interest, and her eyes strayed to the improbable lovers. She said: 'Do you know that story?'

'No,' I said. 'But I can see there has to be one.'

'Though it's not what you think. Uncle Willie could have made something divine out of it. So could Henry James – better than Uncle Willie, because Uncle Willie would have cheated, and for the sake of a movie sale, would have made Delphine and Bobby lovers.'

Delphine Austin from Detroit: I'd read about her in the columns – an heiress married to a marbleized pillar of New York clubman society. Bobby, her companion, was Jewish, the son of hotel magnate S. L. L. Semenenko and first husband of a weird young movie cutie who had divorced him to marry his father (and whom the father had divorced when he caught her *in flagrante* with a German shepherd . . . dog. I'm not kidding).

According to Lady Ina, Delphine Austin and Bobby Semenenko had been inseparable the past year or so, lunching every day at Côte Basque and Lutèce and L'Aiglon, traveling in winter to Gstaad and Lyford Cay, skiing, swimming, spreading themselves with utmost vigor considering the bond was not June-and-January frivolities but really the basis for a double-bill, double-barreled, three-handkerchief variation on an old Bette Davis weeper like *Dark Victory*: they were both dying of leukemia.

'I mean, a worldly woman and a beautiful young man who travel together with death as their common lover and companion. Don't you think Henry James could have done something with that? Or Uncle Willie?'

'No. It's too corny for James, and not corny enough for Maugham.'

'Well, you must admit, Mrs Hopkins would make a fine tale.'

'Who?' I said.

'Standing there,' Ina Coolbirth said.

That Mrs Hopkins. A redhead dressed in black; black hat with a veil trim, a black Mainbocher suit, black crocodile purse, crocodile shoes. M. Soulé had an ear cocked as she stood whispering to him; and suddenly everyone was whispering. Mrs Kennedy and her sister had elicited not a murmur, nor had the entrances of Lauren Bacall and Katharine Cornell and Clare Boothe Luce. However, Mrs Hopkins was *une autre chose*: a sensation to unsettle the suavest Côte Basque client. There was nothing surreptitious in the attention allotted her as she moved with head bowed toward a table where an escort already awaited her – a Catholic priest, one of those highbrow, malnutritional, Father D'Arcy clerics who always seem most at home when absent from the cloisters and while consorting with the very grand and very rich in a wine-and-roses stratosphere.

'Only,' said Lady Ina, 'Ann Hopkins would think of that. To advertise your search for spiritual "advice" in the most public possible manner. Once a tramp, always a tramp.'

'You don't think it was an accident?' I said.

'Come out of the trenches, boy. The war's over. Of course it wasn't an accident. She killed David with malice aforethought. She's a murderess. The police know that.'

'Then how did she get away with it?'

'Because the family wanted her to. David's family. And, as it happened in Newport, old Mrs Hopkins had the power to prevail. Have you ever met David's mother? Hilda Hopkins?'

'I saw her once last summer in Southampton. She was buying a pair of tennis shoes. I wondered what a woman her age, she must be eighty, wanted with tennis shoes. She looked like ... some very old goddess.'

'She is. That's why Ann Hopkins got away with cold-blooded murder. Her mother-in-law is a Rhode Island goddess. *And* a saint.'

Ann Hopkins had lifted her veil and was now whispering to the priest, who, servilely entranced, was brushing a Gibson against his starved blue lips.

'But it *could* have been an accident. If one goes by the papers. As I remember, they'd just come home 59 from a dinner party in Watch Hill and gone to bed in separate rooms. Weren't there supposed to have been a recent series of burglaries thereabouts? – and she kept a shotgun by her bed, and suddenly in the dark her bedroom door opened and she grabbed the shotgun and shot at what she thought was a prowler. Only it was her husband. David Hopkins. With a hole through his head.'

'That's what she said. That's what her lawyer said. That's what the police said. And that's what the papers said ... even the *Times*. But that isn't what happened.' And Ina, inhaling like a skin diver, began: 'Once upon a time a jazzy little carrot-top killer rolled into town from Wheeling or Logan – somewhere in West Virginia. She was eighteen, she'd been brought up in some country-slum way, and she had already been married and divorced; or she *said* she'd been married a month or two to a marine and divorced him when he disappeared (keep that in mind: it's an important clue). Her name was Ann Cutler, and she looked rather like a malicious Betty Grable. She worked as a call girl for a pimp who was a bell captain at the Waldorf; and she saved her money and took voice lessons and dance lessons and ended up as the favorite lay of one of Frankie

Costello's shysters, and he always took her to El Morocco. It was during the war – 1943 – and Elmer's was always full of gangsters and military brass. But one night an ordinary young marine showed up there; except that he wasn't ordinary: his father was one of the stuffiest men in the East – and richest. David had sweetness and great good looks, but he was just like old Mr Hopkins really – an anal-oriented Episcopalian. Stingy. Sober. Not at all café society. But there he was at Elmer's, a soldier on leave, horny, and a bit stoned. One of Winchell's stooges was there, and he recognized the Hopkins boy; he bought David a drink, and said he could fix it up for him with any one of the girls he saw, just pick one, and David, poor sod, said the redhead with the button nose and big tits was okay by him. So the Winchell stooge sends her a note, and at dawn little David finds himself writhing inside the grip of an expert Cleopatra's clutch.

'I'm sure it was David's first experience with anything less primitive than a belly rub with his prep-school roomie. He went bonkers, not that one can blame him; I know some very grown-up Mr Cool Balls who've gone bonkers over Ann Hopkins. She was clever with David; she knew she'd hooked a biggie, even if he was only a kid, so she quit what she was doing and got a job in lingerie at Saks; she never pressed for anything, refused any gift fancier than a handbag, and all the while he was in the service she wrote him every day, little letters cozy and innocent as a baby's layette. In fact, she *was* knocked up; and it *was* his kid; but she didn't tell him a thing until he next came home on leave and found his girl four months pregnant. Now, here is where she showed that certain venomous *élan* that separates truly dangerous serpents from mere chicken snakes: she told him she didn't want to marry him. Wouldn't marry him under any circumstances because she had no desire to lead a Hopkins life; she had neither the background nor innate ability to cope with it, and she was sure neither his family nor friends would ever accept her. She said all she would ever ask would be a modest amount of child support. David protested, but of course he was relieved, even though he would still have to go to his father with the story – David had no money of his own.

'It was then that Ann made her smartest move; she had been doing her homework, and she knew everything there was to know about David's parents; so she said: 'David, there's just one thing I'd like. I want to meet your family. I never had much family of my own, and I'd like my child to have some occasional contact with his grandparents. They might like that, too." *C'est très joli, très diabolique, non?* And it worked. Not that Mr Hopkins was fooled. Right from the start he said the girl was a tramp, and she would never see a nickel of his; but Hilda Hopkins fell for it – she believed that gorgeous hair and those blue malarkey eyes, the whole poor-little-match-girl pitch Ann was tossing her. And as David was the oldest son, and she was in a hurry for a grandchild, she did exactly what Ann had gambled on: she persuaded David to marry her, and her husband to, if not condone it, at least not forbid it. And for some while it seemed as if Mrs Hopkins had been very wise: each year she was rewarded with another grandchild until there were three, two girls and a boy; and Ann's social pickup was incredibly quick – she crashed right through, not bothering to observe any speed limits. She certainly grasped the essentials, I'll say that. She learned to ride and became the horsiest horse-hag in Newport. She studied French and had a French butler and campaigned for the Best Dressed List by lunching with Eleanor Lambert and inviting her for weekends. She learned about furniture and fabrics from Sister Parish and Billy Baldwin; and little Henry Geldzahler was pleased to come to tea (Tea! Ann Cutler! My God!) and to talk to her about modern paintings.

'But the deciding element in her success, leaving aside the fact she'd married a great Newport name, was the duchess. Ann realized something that only the cleverest social climbers ever do. If you want to ride swiftly and safely from the depths to the surface, the surest way is to single out a shark and attach yourself to it like a pilot fish. This is as true in Keokuk, where one massages, say, the local Mrs Ford Dealer, as it is in Detroit, where you may as well try for Mrs Ford herself – or in Paris or Rome. But why should Ann Hopkins, being by marriage a Hopkins and the daughter-in-law of *the* Hilda Hopkins, need the duchess? Because she needed the blessing of someone with presumably high standards, someone with international impact whose acceptance of her would silence the laughing hyenas. And who better than the duchess? As for the duchess, she has high tolerance for the flattery of rich ladies-in-waiting, the kind who always pick up the check; I wonder if the duchess has *ever* picked up a check. Not that it matters. She gives good value. She's one of that unusual female breed who are able to have a genuine friendship with another woman. Certainly she was a marvelous friend to Ann Hopkins. Of course, she wasn't taken in by Ann – after all, the duchess is too much of a con artist not to twig another one; but the idea amused her of taking this cool-eyed cardplayer and lacquering her with a little real style, launching her on the circuit, and the young Mrs Hopkins became quite notorious – though without the style. The father of the second Hopkins girl was Fon Portago, or so everyone says, and God knows she does look very *espagnole*; however that may be, Ann Hopkins was definitely racing her motor in the Grand Prix manner.

'One summer she and David took a house at Cap Ferrat (she was trying to worm her way in with Uncle Willie: she even learned to play first-class bridge; but Uncle Willie said that while she was a woman he might enjoy writing about, she was not someone he trusted to have at his card table), and from Nice to Monte she was known by every male past puberty as Madame Marmalade – her favorite *petit déjeuner* being hot cock buttered with Dundee's best. Although I'm told it's actually strawberry jam she prefers. I don't think David guessed the full 65 measure of these fandangos, but there was no doubt he was miserable, and after a while he fell in with the very girl he ought to have married originally – his second cousin, Mary Kendall, no beauty but a sensible, attractive girl who had always been in love with him. She was engaged to Tommy Bedford but broke it off when David asked her to marry him. *If* he could get a divorce. And he *could*; all it would cost him, according to Ann, was five million dollars tax-free. David still had no glue of his own, and when he took this proposition to his father, Mr Hopkins said *never!* and said he'd always warned that Ann was what she was, bad baggage, but David hadn't listened, so now that was his burden, and as long as the father lived she would never get a subway token. After this, David hired a detective and within six months had enough evidence, including Polaroids of her being screwed front and back by a couple of jockeys in Saratoga, to have her jailed, much less divorce her. But when David confronted her, Ann laughed and told him his father would never allow him to take such filth into court. She was right. It was interesting, because when discussing the matter, Mr Hopkins told David that, under the circum-

stances, he wouldn't object to the son killing the

wife, then keeping his mouth shut, but certainly David couldn't divorce her and supply the press with that kind of manure.

'It was at this point that David's detective had an inspiration; an unfortunate one, because if it had never come about, David might still be alive. However, the detective had an idea: he searched out the Cutler homestead in West Virginia — or was it Kentucky? — and interviewed relatives who had never heard from her after she'd gone to New York, had never known her in her grand incarnation as Mrs David Hopkins but simply as Mrs Billy Joe Barnes, the wife of a hillbilly jarhead. The detective got a copy of the marriage certificate from the local courthouse, and after that he tracked down this Billy Joe Barnes, found him working as an airplane mechanic in San Diego, and persuaded him to sign an affidavit saying he had married one Ann Cutler, never divorced her, not remarried, that he simply had returned from Okinawa to find she had disappeared, but as far as he knew she was still Mrs Billy Joe Barnes. Indeed she was! — even the cleverest criminal minds have a basic stupidity. And when David presented her with the information and said to her: "Now we'll have no more of those round-figure ultimatums, since we're not legally married," surely it was then she decided to kill him: a decision made by her genes, the inescapable white-trash slut inside her, even though she knew the Hopkinses would arrange a respectable "divorce" and provide a very good allowance; but she also knew if she murdered David, and got away with it, she and her children would eventually receive his inheritance, something that wouldn't happen if he married Mary Kendall and had a second family.

'So she pretended to acquiesce and told David there was no point arguing as he obviously had her by the snatch, but would he continue to live with her for a month while she settled her affairs? He agreed, idiot; and immediately she began preparing the legend of the prowler – twice she called police, claiming a prowler was on the grounds; soon she had the servants and most of the neighbors convinced that prowlers were everywhere in the vicinity, and actually, Nini Wolcott's house was broken into, presumably by a burglar, but now even Nini admits that Ann must have done it. As you may recall, if you followed the case, the Hopkinses went to a party at the Wolcotts' the night it happened. A Labor Day dinner dance with about fifty guests; I was there, and I sat next to David at dinner. He seemed very relaxed, full of smiles, I suppose because he thought he'd soon be rid of the bitch and married to his cousin Mary; but Ann was wearing a pale-green dress, and she seemed almost green with tension – she chattered on like a lunatic chimpanzee about prowlers and burglars and how she always slept now with a shotgun by her bedside. According to the *Times*, David and Ann left the Wolcotts' a bit after midnight, and when they reached home, where the servants were on holiday and the children staying with their grandparents in Bar Harbor, they retired to separate bedrooms. Ann's story was, and is, that she went straight to sleep but was awakened within half an hour by the noise of her bedroom door opening: she saw a shadowy figure – the prowler! She grabbed her shotgun and in the dark fired away, emptying both barrels. Then she turned on the lights and, oh, horror of horrors, discovered David sprawled in the hallway nicely cooled. But that isn't where the cops found him. Because that isn't where or how he was killed. The police found the body inside a glassed-in shower, naked. The water was still running, and the shower door was shattered with bullets.'

'In other words –' I began.

'In other words' – Lady Ina picked up but waited until a captain, supervised by a perspiring M. Soulé, had finished ladling out the soufflé Furstenberg – 'none of Ann's story was true. God knows what she expected people to believe; but she just, after they reached home and David had stripped to take a shower, followed him there with a gun and shot him through the shower door. Perhaps she intended to say the prowler had stolen her shotgun and killed him. In that case, why didn't she call a doctor, call the police? Instead, she telephoned her *lawyer*. Yes. And *he* called the police. But not until *after* he had called the Hopkinses in Bar Harbor.'

The priest was swilling another Gibson; Ann Hopkins, head bent, was still whispering at him confessionally. Her waxy fingers, unpainted and unadorned except for a stark gold wedding band, nibbled at her breast as though she were reading rosary beads.

'But if the police *knew* the truth –'

'Of course they knew.'

'Then I don't see how she got away with it. It's not conceivable.'

'I told you,' Ina said tartly, 'she got away with it because Hilda Hopkins wanted her to. It was the children: tragic enough to have lost their father,

what purpose could it serve to see the mother con-
victed of murder? Hilda Hopkins, and old Mr
Hopkins, too, wanted Ann to go scot-free; and the
Hopkinses, within their terrain, have the power to
brainwash cops, reweave minds, move corpses from
shower stalls to hallways; the power to control in-
quests – David's death was declared an accident at
an inquest that lasted less than a day.' She looked
across at Ann Hopkins and her companion – the
latter, his clerical brow scarlet with a two-cocktail
flush, not listening now to the imploring murmur of
his patroness but staring rather glassy-gaga at Mrs
Kennedy, as if any moment he might run amok and
ask her to autograph a menu. 'Hilda's behavior has
been extraordinary. Flawless. One would never sus-
pect she wasn't truly the affectionate, grieving protec-
tor of a bereaved and very legitimate widow. She
never gives a dinner party without inviting her. The
one thing I wonder is what everyone wonders
when they're alone, just the two of them, what do
they talk about?' Ina selected from her salad a leaf of
Bibb lettuce, pinned it to a fork, studied it through
her black spectacles. 'There is at least one respect in
which the rich, the really very rich, *are* different
from . . . other people. They understand *vegetables*. 71

Other people – well, anyone can manage roast beef, a great steak, lobsters. But have you ever noticed how, in the homes of the very rich, at the Wrightsmans' or Dillons', at Bunny's and Babe's, they always serve only the most beautiful vegetables, and the greatest variety? The greenest *petits pois*, infinitesimal carrots, corn so baby-kerneled and tender it seems almost unborn, lima beans tinier than mice eyes, and the young asparagus! The limestone lettuce! The raw red mushrooms! Zucchini . . .' Lady Ina was feeling her champagne.

Mrs Matthau and Mrs Cooper lingered over *café filtre.* 'I know,' mused Mrs Matthau, who was analyzing the wife of a midnight-TV clown/hero, 'Jane *is* pushy: all those telephone calls – Christ, she could dial Answer Prayer and talk an hour. But she's bright, she's fast on the draw, and when you think what she has to put with. This last episode she told me about: hair-raising. Well, Bobby had a week off from the show – he was so exhausted he told Jane he wanted just to stay home, spend the whole week slopping around in his pajamas, and Jane was ecstatic; she bought hundreds of magazines and books and new LPs and every kind of goody from Maison

Glass. Oh, it was going to be a lovely week. Just Jane and Bobby sleeping and screwing and having baked potatoes with caviar for breakfast. But after one day he evaporated. Didn't come home that night or call. It wasn't the first time, Jesus be, but Jane was out of her mind. Still, she couldn't report it to the police; what a sensation that would be. Another day passed, and not a word. Jane hadn't slept for forty-eight hours. Around three in the morning the phone rang. Bobby. Smashed. She said: "My God, Bobby, where are you?" He said he was in Miami, and she said, losing her temper now, how the fuck did you get in Miami, and he said, oh, he'd gone to the airport and taken a plane, and she said what the fuck for, and he said just because he felt like being alone. Jane said: "And *are* you alone?" Bobby, you know what a sadist he is behind that huckleberry grin, said: "No. There's someone lying right here. She'd like to speak to you." And on comes this scared little giggling peroxide voice: "Really, is this really Mrs Baxter, hee hee? I thought Bobby was making a funny, hee hee. We just heard on the radio how it was snowing there in New York – I mean, you ought to be down here with us where it's ninety degrees!" Jane said, very chiseled: "I'm afraid I'm much too ill to travel." 73

And peroxide, all fluttery distress: "Oh, gee, I'm sorry to hear that. What's the matter, honey?" Jane said: "I've got a double dose of syph and the old clap-clap, all courtesy of that great comic, my husband, Bobby Baxter – and if you don't want the same, I suggest you get the hell out of there." And she hung up.'

Mrs Cooper was amused, though not very; puzzled, rather. 'How can any women tolerate that? I'd divorce him.'

'Of course you would. But then, you've got the two things Jane hasn't.'

'Ah?'

'One: dough. And two: identity.'

Lady Ina was ordering another bottle of Cristal. 'Why not?' she asked, defiantly replying to my concerned expression. 'Easy up, Jonesy. You won't have to carry me piggyback. I just feel like it: shattering the day into golden pieces.' Now, I thought, she's going to tell me what she wants, but doesn't want, to tell me. But no, not yet. Instead: 'Would you care to hear a truly vile story? Really vomitous? Then look to your left. That sow sitting next to Betsy Whitney.'

She *was* somewhat porcine, a swollen muscular baby with a freckled Bahamas-burnt face and squinty-mean eyes; she looked as if she wore tweed brassières and played a lot of golf.

'The governor's wife?'

'The governor's wife,' said Ina, nodding as she gazed with melancholy contempt at the homely beast, legal spouse of a former New York governor. 'Believe it or not, but one of the most attractive guys who ever filled a pair of trousers used to get a hard-on every time he looked at that bull dyke. Sidney Dillon —' the name, pronounced by Ina, was a caressing hiss.

To be sure. Sidney Dillon. Conglomateur, adviser to Presidents, an old flame of Ina's. I remember once picking up a copy of what was, after the Bible and *The Murder of Roger Ackroyd*, Ina's favorite book, Isak Dinesen's *Out of Africa*; from between the pages fell a Polaroid picture of a swimmer standing at water's edge, a wiry well-constructed man with a hairy chest and a twinkle-grinning tough-Jew face; his bathing trunks were rolled to his knees, one hand rested sexily on a hip, and with the other he was pumping a dark fat mouth-watering dick. On the reverse side a notation, made in Ina's boyish script, read: *Sidney. Lago di Garda. En route to Venice. June, 1962.*

'Dill and I have always told each other everything. He was my lover for two years when I was just out of college and working at *Harper's Bazaar.* The only thing he ever specifically asked me never to repeat was this business about the governor's wife; I'm a bitch to tell it, and maybe I wouldn't if it wasn't for all these blissful bubbles risin' in my noggin –' She lifted her champagne and peered at me through its sunny effervescence. 'Gentlemen, the question is: why would an educated, dynamic, very rich and well-hung Jew go bonkers for a cretinous Protestant size forty who wears low-heeled shoes and lavender water? Especially when he's married to Cleo Dillon, to my mind the most beautiful creature alive, always excepting the Garbo of even ten years ago (incidentally, I saw her last night at the P. B. Gunthers', and I must say the whole setup has taken on a very weathered look, dry and drafty, like an abandoned temple, something lost in the jungles at Angkor Wat; but that's what happens when you spend most of a life loving only yourself, and that not very much).

'Dill's in his sixties now; he could still have any woman he wants, yet for years he yearned after yonder porco. I'm sure he never entirely understood this ultra-perversion, the reason for it; or if he did, he never would admit it, not even to an analyst – that's a thought! Dill at an analyst! Men like that can never be analyzed because they don't consider any other man their equal. But as for the governor's wife, it was simply that for Dill she was the living incorporation of everything denied him, forbidden to him as a Jew, no matter how beguiling and rich he might be: the Racquet Club, Le Jockey, the Links, White's – all those places he would never sit down to a table of backgammon, all those golf courses where he would never sink a putt – the Everglades and the Seminole, the Maidstone, and St Paul's and St Mark's, *et al.*, the saintly little New England schools his sons would never attend. Whether he confesses to it or not, that's why he wanted to fuck the governor's wife, revenge himself on that smug hog-bottom, make her sweat and squeal and call him daddy. He kept his distance, though, and never hinted at any interest in the lady, but waited for the moment when the stars were in their correct constellation. It came unplanned – one night he went to a dinner party at the Cowleses'; Cleo had gone to a wedding in Boston. The governor's wife was seated next to him at dinner; 77

she, too, had come alone, the governor off campaigning somewhere. Dill joked, he dazzled; she sat there pig-eyed and indifferent, but she didn't seem surprised when he rubbed his leg against hers, and when he asked if he might see her home, she nodded, not with much enthusiasm but with a decisiveness that made him feel she was ready to accept whatever he proposed.

'At that time Dill and Cleo were living in Greenwich; they'd sold their town house on Riverview Terrace and had only a two-room *pied-à-terre* at the Pierre, just a living room and a bedroom. In the car, after they'd left the Cowleses', he suggested they stop by the Pierre for a nightcap: he wanted her opinion of his new Bonnard. She said she would be pleased to give her opinion; and why shouldn't the idiot have one? Wasn't her husband on the board of directors at the Modern? When she'd seen the painting, he offered her a drink, and she said she'd like a brandy; she sip-sipped it, sitting opposite him across a coffee table, nothing at all happening between them, except that suddenly she was very talkative – about the horse sales in Saratoga, and a hole-by-hole golf game she'd played with Doc Holden at Lyford Cay; she talked about how the dentist she'd used since she was a little girl had died and now she didn't know *what* to do with her teeth; oh, she jabbered on until it was almost two, and Dill kept looking at his watch, not only because he'd had a long day and was anxious but because he expected Cleo back on an early plane from Boston: she'd said she would see him at the Pierre before he left for the office. So eventually, while she was rattling on about root canals, he shut her up: "Excuse me, my dear, but do you want to fuck or not?" There is something to be said for aristocrats, even the stupidest have had some kind of class bred into them; so she shrugged – "Well, yes, I suppose so" – as though a salesgirl had asked if she liked the look of a hat. Merely resigned, as it were, to that old familiar hard-sell Jewish effrontery.

'In the bedroom she asked him not to turn on the lights. She was quite firm about that – and in view of what finally transpired, one can scarcely blame her. They undressed in the dark, and she took forever – unsnapping, untying, unzipping – and said not a word except to remark on the fact that the Dillons obviously slept in the same bed, since there was only the one; and he told her yes, he was affectionate, a mama's boy who couldn't sleep unless he had something soft to cuddle against. The governor's wife was neither a cuddler nor a kisser. Kissing her, according to Dill, was like playing post office with a dead and rotting whale: she really did need a dentist. None of his tricks caught her fancy, she just lay there, inert, like a missionary being outraged by a succession of sweating Swahilis. Dill couldn't come. He felt as though he was sloshing around in some strange puddle, the whole ambience so slippery he couldn't get a proper grip. He thought maybe if he went down on her – but the moment he started to, she hauled him up by his hair: "Nonononono, for God's sake, don't do that!" Dill gave up, he rolled over, he said: "I don't suppose you'd blow me?" She didn't bother to reply, so he said okay, all right, just jack me off and we'll call it scratch, okay? But she was already up, and she asked him please not to turn on the light, please, and she said no, he need not see her home, stay where he was, go to sleep, and while he lay there listening to her dress he reached down to finger himself, and it felt . . . it felt . . . He jumped up and snapped on the light. His whole paraphernalia had felt sticky and strange. As though it were covered with blood. As it was. So was the bed. The sheets

bloodied with stains the size of Brazil. The governor's

wife had just picked up her purse, had just opened the door, and Dill said: "What the hell is this? Why did you do it?" Then he knew why, not because she told him, but because of the glance he caught as she closed the door: like Carino, the cruel maître d' at the old Elmer's – leading some blue-suit brown-shoes hunker to a table in Siberia. She had mocked him, punished him for his Jewish presumption.

'Jonesy, you're not eating?'

'It isn't doing much for my appetite. This conversation.'

'As I warned you it was a vile story. And we haven't come to the best part yet.'

'All right. I'm ready.'

'No, Jonesy. Not if it's going to make you sick.'

'I'll take my chances,' I said.

Mrs Kennedy and her sister had left; the governor's wife was leaving, Soulé beaming and bobbing in her wide-hipped wake. Mrs Matthau and Mrs Cooper were still present but silent, their ears perked to our conversation; Mrs Matthau was kneading a fallen yellow rose petal – her fingers stiffened as Ina resumed: 'Poor Dill didn't realize the extent of his difficulties until he'd stripped the sheets off the bed 81 and found there were no clean ones to replace them. Cleo, you see, used the Pierre's linen and kept none of her own at the hotel. It was three o'clock in the morning and he couldn't reasonably call for maid service: what would he say, how could he explain the loss of his sheets at that hour? The particular hell of it was that Cleo would be sailing in from Boston in a matter of hours, and regardless how much Dill screwed around, he'd always been scrupulous about never giving Cleo a clue; he really loved her, and, my God, what could he say when she saw that bed? He took a cold shower and tried to think of some buddy he could call and ask to hustle over with a change of sheets. There was me, of course; he trusted *me*, but I was in London. And there was his old valet, Wardell. Wardell was queer for Dill and had been a slave for twenty years just for the privilege of soaping him whenever Dill took his bath; but Wardell was old and arthritic, Dill *couldn't* call him in Greenwich and ask him to drive all the way in to town. Then it struck him that he had a hundred chums but really no friends, not the kind you ring at three in the morning. In his own company he employed more than six thousand people, but there was not one who had ever called him anything except *Mr Dillon*. I mean, the guy was feeling sorry for himself. So he poured a truly stiff Scotch and started searching in the kitchen for a box of laundry soap, but he couldn't find any, and in the end had to use a bar of Guerlain's *Fleurs des Alpes.* To wash the sheets. He soaked them in the tub in scalding water. Scrubbed and scrubbed. Rinsed and scrubadubdubbed. There he was, the powerful Mr Dillon, down on his knees and flogging away like a Spanish peasant at the side of the stream.

'It was five o'clock, it was six, the sweat poured off him, he felt as if he were trapped in a sauna; he said the next day when he weighed himself he'd lost eleven pounds. Full daylight was upon him before the sheets looked incredibly white. But wet. He wondered if hanging them out of the window might help – or merely attract the police? At last he thought of drying them in the kitchen oven. It was only one of those little hotel stoves, but he stuffed them in and set them to bake at four hundred fifty degrees. And they baked, brother: smoked and steamed – the bastard burned his hand pulling them out. Now it was eight o'clock and there was no time left. So he decided there was nothing to do but make up the bed with the steamy soggy sheets, climb between 83 them and say his prayers. He really *was* praying when he started to snore. When he woke up it was noon, and there was a note on the bureau from Cleo: "Darling, you were sleeping so soundly and sweetly that I just tiptoed in and changed and have gone on to Greenwich. Hurry home."'

The Mesdames Cooper and Matthau, having heard their fill, self-consciously prepared to depart.

Mrs Cooper said: 'D–darling, there's the most m–m–marvelous auction at Parke Bernet this afternoon – Gothic tapestries.'

'What the fuck,' asked Mrs Matthau, 'would I do with a Gothic tapestry?'

Mrs Cooper replied: 'I thought they might be amusing for picnics at the beach. You know, spread them on the sands.'

Lady Ina, after extracting from her purse a Bulgari vanity case made of white enamel sprinkled with diamond flakes, an object remindful of snow prisms, was dusting her face with a powder-puff. She started with her chin, moved to her nose, and the next thing I knew she was slapping away at the lenses of her dark glasses.

And I said: 'What are you doing, Ina?'

She said: 'Damn! Damn!' and pulled off the glasses

and mopped them with a napkin. A tear had slid down to dangle like sweat at the tip of a nostril – not a pretty sight; neither were her eyes – red and veined from a heap of sleepless weeping. 'I'm on my way to Mexico to get a divorce.'

One wouldn't have thought that would make her unhappy; her husband was the stateliest bore in England, an ambitious achievement, considering some of the competition: the Earl of Derby, the Duke of Marlborough, to name but two. Certainly that was Lady Ina's opinion; still, I could understand why she married him – he was rich, he was technically alive, he was a 'good gun' and for that reason reigned in hunting circles, boredom's Valhalla. Whereas Ina . . . Ina was fortyish and a multiple divorcée on the rebound from an affair with a Rothschild who had been satisfied with her as a mistress but hadn't thought her grand enough to wed. So Ina's friends were relieved when she returned from a shoot in Scotland engaged to Lord Coolbirth; true, the man was humorless, dull, sour as port decanted too long – but, all said and done, a lucrative catch.

'I know what you're thinking,' Ina remarked, amid more tearful trickling. 'That if I'm getting a good settlement, I ought to be congratulated. I don't deny Cool was tough to take. Like living with a suit of armor. But I did . . . feel safe. For the first time I felt I had a man I couldn't possibly lose. Who else would want him? But I've now learned this, Jonesy, and hark me well: there's always someone around to pick up an old husband. *Always*.' A crescendo of hiccups interrupted her: M. Soulé, observing from a concealed distance, pursed his lips. 'I was careless. Lazy. But I just couldn't bear any more of those wet Scottish weekends with the bullets whizzing round, so he started going alone, and after a while I began to notice that everywhere he went Elda Morris was sure to go – whether it was a grouse shoot in the Hebrides or a boar hunt in Yugoslavia. She even tagged along to Spain when Franco gave that huge hunting party last October. But I didn't make too much of it – Elda's a great gun, but she's also a hard-boiled fifty-year-old virgin; I *still* can't conceive of Cool wanting to get into those rusty knickers.'

Her hand weaved towards the champagne glass, but without arriving at its destination, drooped and fell like a drunk suddenly sprawling flat on the street. 'Two weeks ago,' she began, her voice slowed, her Montana accent becoming more manifest, 'as 86 Cool and I were winging to New York, I realized

that he was staring at me with a, hmnnn, *ser*pentine
scowl. Ordinarily he looks like an egg. It was only
nine in the morning; nevertheless, we were drinking
that loathsome airplane champagne, and when we'd
finished a bottle and I saw he was still looking at me
in this . . . homicidal . . . way, I said: "What's bug-
ging you, Cool?" And *he* said: "Nothing that a
divorce from you wouldn't cure." Imagine the wicked-
ness of it! springing something like that on a plane! –
when you're stuck together for hours, and can't get
away, can't shout or scream. It was doubly nasty of
him because he knows I'm terrified of flying – he
knew I was full of pills and booze. So now I'm on my
way to Mexico.' At last her hand retrieved the glass of
Cristal; she sighed, a sound despondent as spiraling
autumn leaves. 'My kind of woman needs a man.
Not for sex. Oh, I like a good screw. But I've had
my share; I can do without it. But I can't live
without a man. Women like me have no other focus,
no other way of scheduling our lives; even if we hate
him, even if he's an iron head with a cotton heart,
it's better than this footloose routine. Freedom may
be the most important thing in life, but there's such
a thing as too much freedom. And I'm the wrong age
now, I can't face all that again, the long hunt, the 87

sitting up all night at Elmer's or Annabel's with some fat greaser swimming in a sea of stingers. All the old gal pals asking you to their little black-tie dinners and not really wanting an extra woman and wondering where they're going to find a "suitable" extra man for an aging broad like Ina Coolbirth. As though there *were* any suitable extra men in New York. *Or* London. Or Butte, Montana, if it comes to that. They're all queer. Or *ought* to be. That's what I meant when I told Princess Margaret it was too bad she didn't like fags because it meant she would have a very lonely old age. Fags are the only people who are kind to worldly old women; and I adore them, I always have, but I really am not *ready* to become a full-time fag's moll; I'd rather go dyke.

'No, Jonesy, that's never been part of my repertoire, but I can see the appeal for a woman my age, someone who can't abide loneliness, who needs comfort and admiration: some dykes can ladle it out good. There's nothing cozier or safer than a nice little lez-nest. I remember when I saw Anita Hohnsbeen in Sante Fe. How I envied her. But I've always envied Anita. She was a senior at Sarah Lawrence when I was a freshman. I think everyone had a crush on Anita. She wasn't beautiful, even pretty, but she was so bright and nerveless and *clean* — her hair, her skin, she always looked like the first morning on earth. If she hadn't had all that glue, and if that climbing Southern mother of hers had stopped pushing her, I think she would have married an archaeologist and spent a happy lifetime excavating urns in Anatolia. But why disinter Anita's wretched history? — five husbands and one retarded child, just a waste until she'd had several hundred breakdowns and weighed ninety pounds and her doctor sent her out to Santa Fe. Did you know Santa Fe is the dyke capital of the United States? What San Francisco is to *les garçons*, Sante Fe is to the Daughters of Bilitis. I suppose it's because the butchier ones like dragging up in boots and denim. There's a delicious woman there, Megan O'Meaghan, and Anita met her and, baby, that was *it*. All she'd ever needed was a good pair of motherly tits to suckle. Now she and Megan live in a rambling adobe in the foothills, and Anita looks . . . almost as clear-eyed as she did when we were at school together. Oh, it's a bit corny — the piñon fires, the Indian fetish dolls, Indian rugs, and the two ladies fussing in the kitchen over homemade tacos and the "perfect" Margarita. But say what you will, 89 it's one of the pleasantest homes I've ever been in. Lucky Anita!'

She lurched upward, a dolphin shattering the surface of the sea, pushed back the table (overturning a champagne glass), seized her purse, said: 'Be right back'; and careened toward the mirrored door of the Côte Basque powder room.

Although the priest and the assassin were still whispering and sipping at their table, the restaurant's rooms had emptied, M. Soulé had retired. Only the hatcheck girl and a few waiters impatiently flicking napkins remained. Stewards were resetting the tables, sprucing the flowers for the evening visitors. It was an atmosphere of luxurious exhaustion, like a ripened, shedding rose, while all that waited outside was the failing New York afternoon.

READ MORE IN PENGUIN

For complete information about books available from Penguin and how to order them, please write to us at the appropriate address below. Please note that for copyright reasons the selection of books varies from country to country.

IN THE UNITED KINGDOM: Please write to *Dept. JC, Penguin Books Ltd, FREEPOST, West Drayton, Middlesex UB7 0BR.*

If you have any difficulty in obtaining a title, please send your order with the correct money, plus ten per cent for postage and packaging, to *PO Box No. 11, West Drayton, Middlesex UB7 0BR.*

IN THE UNITED STATES: Please write to *Consumer Sales, Penguin USA, P.O. Box 999, Dept. 17109, Bergenfield, New Jersey 07621-0120.* VISA and MasterCard holders call 1-800-253-6476 to order all Penguin titles.

IN CANADA: Please write to *Penguin Books Canada Ltd, 10 Alcorn Avenue, Suite 300, Toronto, Ontario M4V 3B2.*

IN AUSTRALIA: Please write to *Penguin Books Australia Ltd, P.O. Box 257, Ringwood, Victoria 3134.*

IN NEW ZEALAND: Please write to *Penguin Books (NZ) Ltd, Private Bag 102902, North Shore Mail Centre, Auckland 10.*

IN INDIA: Please write to *Penguin Books India Pvt Ltd, 706 Eros Apartments, 56 Nehru Place, New Delhi 110 019.*

IN THE NETHERLANDS: Please write to *Penguin Books Netherlands bv, Postbus 3507, NL-1001 AH Amsterdam.*

IN GERMANY: Please write to *Penguin Books Deutschland GmbH, Metzlerstrasse 26, 60594 Frankfurt am Main.*

IN SPAIN: Please write to *Penguin Books S. A., Bravo Murillo 19, 1o B, 28015 Madrid.*

IN ITALY: Please write to *Penguin Italia s.r.l., Via Felice Casati 20, I-20124 Milano.*

IN FRANCE: Please write to *Penguin France S. A., 17 rue Lejeune, F-31000 Toulouse.*

IN JAPAN: Please write to *Penguin Books Japan, Ishikiribashi Building, 2-5-4, Suido, Bunkyo-ku, Tokyo 112.*

IN GREECE: Please write to *Penguin Hellas Ltd, Dimocritou 3, GR-106 71 Athens.*

IN SOUTH AFRICA: Please write to *Longman Penguin Southern Africa (Pty) Ltd, Private Bag X08, Bertsham 2013.*